FROSTY'S
~ SNOWY DAY ~

Manufactured in USA.

8   7   6   5   4   3   2   1

ISBN 1-56173-712-7

Contributing writer: Carolyn Quattrocki

Cover illustration: Linda Graves

Book illustrations: Susan Spellman

Publications International, Ltd.

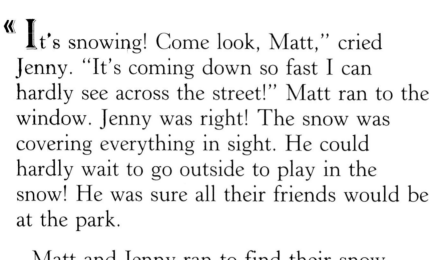

« It's snowing! Come look, Matt," cried Jenny. "It's coming down so fast I can hardly see across the street!" Matt ran to the window. Jenny was right! The snow was covering everything in sight. He could hardly wait to go outside to play in the snow! He was sure all their friends would be at the park.

Matt and Jenny ran to find their snow boots. "I want to come, too!" said Marianna. She always wanted to go wherever they went. "No," said Matt. "You're too little to go to the park with us now. Maybe later."

Jenny and Matt hurried to put on hats, mittens, and scarves. They called goodbye to their mother and raced out the door.

Lisa, Tracy, and Paul were already at the park by the time Matt and Jenny got there. "Isn't this the greatest?" said Tracy. "The snow's so deep!" "Let's build a snowman," said Paul. "A huge snowman—as tall as we can make him."

They got to work. It wasn't easy. They had to roll one great big snowball for his body, another for his chest, and then a smaller one for his head. Then Jenny said, "He needs a face and some clothes." Everyone ran home to see what they could find.

Lisa found some bright, black pieces of coal for his eyes and a button for his nose. Tracy borrowed her big brother's purple scarf, and Paul brought the toy corncob pipe from his Halloween costume.

Matt and Jenny found an old pair of boots. Then they saw Marianna playing with the best thing of all! She had helped Mother clean out the attic and had found a black silk top hat—perfect for their snowman! "Marianna, you can bring the hat for our snowman," said Jenny. "It will help dress him up."

When they all arrived back at the park, Lisa put the button nose and coal eyes on the snowman's face. Tracy wrapped the purple scarf around his neck. And Paul stuck the corncob pipe in his mouth.

Everyone cheered as Paul and Jenny put the hat on their snowman's head. "What shall we name him?" asked Tracy. "How about Frosty?" suggested Jenny. "Yes!" they all cheered.

The children began to dance in a circle around Frosty. Then little Marianna said, "I wish Frosty were alive, so he could play with us." Just then, Matt looked up at Frosty's face. "Oh, my!" he cried. "Frosty just winked at me!"

They all looked just in time to see Frosty smile. He really was alive! "Hooray," they cheered. Then they gave the snowman a big, big hug. Frosty began to laugh. "Hey! I'm ticklish!" he said. "Let go!"

They all laughed, and Frosty began to do a little dance. The children stepped in line behind him. Suddenly there was a grand parade going all around the park, with Frosty leading the way.

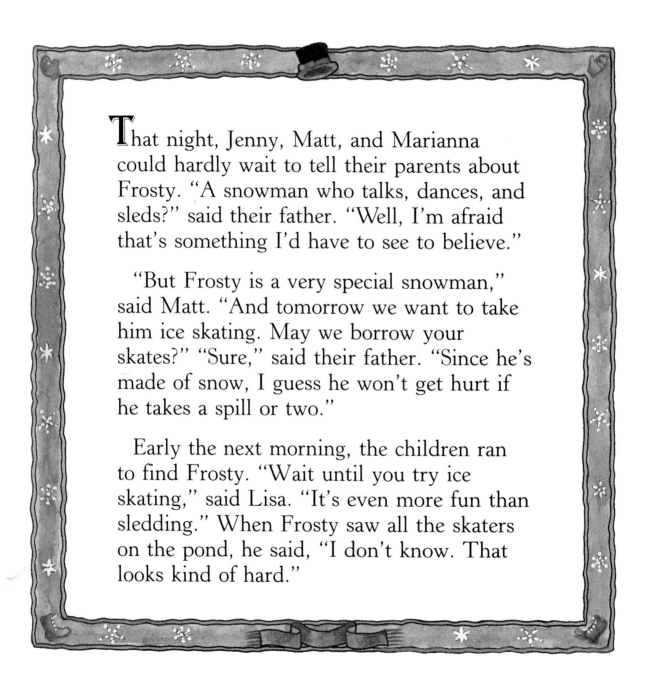

That night, Jenny, Matt, and Marianna could hardly wait to tell their parents about Frosty. "A snowman who talks, dances, and sleds?" said their father. "Well, I'm afraid that's something I'd have to see to believe."

"But Frosty is a very special snowman," said Matt. "And tomorrow we want to take him ice skating. May we borrow your skates?" "Sure," said their father. "Since he's made of snow, I guess he won't get hurt if he takes a spill or two."

Early the next morning, the children ran to find Frosty. "Wait until you try ice skating," said Lisa. "It's even more fun than sledding." When Frosty saw all the skaters on the pond, he said, "I don't know. That looks kind of hard."

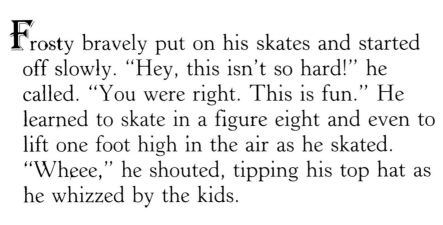

Frosty bravely put on his skates and started off slowly. "Hey, this isn't so hard!" he called. "You were right. This is fun." He learned to skate in a figure eight and even to lift one foot high in the air as he skated. "Wheee," he shouted, tipping his top hat as he whizzed by the kids.

After a while, the children began to get cold. "Come on, Frosty," said Tracy. "Let's go into the warming house and warm up. My hands are freezing."

They stepped into the little warming hut. Their hands and feet began to warm up. But they had forgotten something very important. Frosty was made of snow! "Whew! This place doesn't feel so good to me," he said. "I'll wait outside."

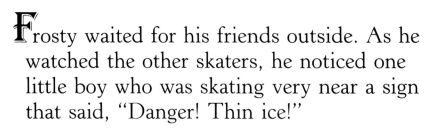

Frosty waited for his friends outside. As he watched the other skaters, he noticed one little boy who was skating very near a sign that said, "Danger! Thin ice!"

"Hey, watch out!" called Frosty. But the little boy didn't hear. He was skating right toward the thin ice! Quick as a wink, Frosty darted out onto the ice after the little boy. Just as the ice started to crack, Frosty caught him by the hand and pulled the boy to safety.

Frosty was a hero! Everyone cheered! "Weren't you scared?" asked Jenny. "What if you had fallen through the ice?" Frosty smiled and said, "You forgot. I'm made of snow. A little cold doesn't bother me!"

The next morning, Jenny looked out the window. "Oh, no!" she said. "It's raining. What will happen to Frosty?" Matt said he thought maybe the rain would stop soon.

But the rain did not stop. It rained all that day. The children watched and worried about their friend Frosty. Finally, the next morning, the rain stopped and the sun came out. "Let's go to the park to see how Frosty is," said Matt. "Come with us, Dad."

When they got to the park, they looked all around. They didn't see Frosty anywhere. Finally, Jenny called out, "Look over there! I see Frosty's hat by the tree." But there was only a little lump of snow next to the hat. Frosty was gone!

They all stood looking at the hat and the little pile of snow. Marianna picked up the hat sadly. Then their father smiled. "Look," he said. "There, under Frosty's hat. He left a promise that he'll be back next year!"

And sure enough, there it was. A little flower, just the color of Frosty's purple scarf, had pushed up through the snow. It almost seemed to smile and say, "See you next year!"